Ninjas Don't
Bake Pumpkin Pies

There are more books about the Bailey School Kids!
Have you read these adventures?

Ninjas Don't Bake Pumpkin Pies

by **Debbie Dadey**
and
Marcia Thornton Jones

illustrated by **John Steven Gurney**

A
LITTLE APPLE
PAPERBACK

SCHOLASTIC INC.
New York   Toronto   London   Auckland   Sydney
Mexico City   New Delhi   Hong Kong

To every orphan — DD

*To my mom, Thelma Kuhljuergen Thornton,
the best cook in the world! — MTJ*

No part of this publication may be reproduced in whole or in part, or stored in a retrieval system, or transmitted in any form or by any means, electronic, mechanical, photocopying, recording, or otherwise, without written permission of the publisher. For information regarding permission, write to Scholastic Inc., Attention: Permissions Department, 555 Broadway, New York, NY 10012.

ISBN 0-439-04398-0

Text copyright © 1999 by Marcia Thornton Jones and Debra S. Dadey.
Illustrations copyright © 1999 by Scholastic Inc.
All rights reserved. Published by Scholastic Inc.
SCHOLASTIC, LITTLE APPLE PAPERBACKS, THE ADVENTURES OF THE BAILEY SCHOOL KIDS, and associated logos are trademarks of Scholastic Inc.
THE ADVENTURES OF THE BAILEY SCHOOL KIDS in design is a registered trademark of Scholastic Inc.

12 11 10 9 8 7 6 5 4 3 2 1   9/9 0 1 2 3 4/0

Printed in the U.S.A.   40

First Scholastic printing, November 1999

Contents

1

Vacation

"This is it!" Eddie shouted after school. He was under the big oak tree on the playground with his friend Liza.

Liza stared at Eddie. He had thrown his backpack down and was trying to do a handstand but was not having very much luck. Mostly he just fell sideways. "That is definitely *not* it," Liza said. "You need to take gymnastics lessons again."

Their friend Melody came up beside them. "This is how you do a handstand," she said. She stood on her hands perfectly for a full minute before jumping back to her feet.

Eddie took off his baseball cap and shook his head. "I don't care about handstands. I just care about getting out of school for vacation."

Melody did another handstand and started singing, "Vacation, all I ever wanted. Vacation, all I ever needed."

Their friend Howie walked up and tried to do a handstand, but he fell right on his face. Eddie helped Howie up from the ground.

Liza pulled her blue wool hat down over her blond hair and shivered in the cool breeze. "You guys better be careful or you'll break your necks before Thanksgiving."

"No more pencils, no more books," Eddie said with a big smile. "No more teacher's dirty looks."

Liza shook her head. "It's not Thanksgiving vacation yet," she told Eddie. "We still have two more days of school left."

Eddie frowned. "Don't remind me."

Melody patted Eddie on the back. "I'm with you," she said. "I feel like celebrating our vacation."

"Why don't we go get a Doodlegum Shake?" Howie suggested.

Liza nodded. "That sounds great," she said. "Let's do it."

Eddie grabbed his backpack and walked down Forest Lane with his friends. They turned the corner onto Main Street and headed toward the ice-cream shop.

"Mmmm," Howie said. "Something smells really good."

Liza's eyes got big and she licked her lips. "I've never smelled anything so wonderful in my whole life."

"Whatever it is," Eddie said, "I've got to get some."

"Doesn't it smell delicious?" Liza asked Melody, but Melody didn't answer.

"Melody?" Liza turned around to ask her friend again. "Melody?"

Melody was gone. Liza looked at Howie and Eddie. "What happened to Melody?" she asked.

"She was with us a minute ago," Howie said with a shrug.

The kids raced back around the corner

and almost ran right into Melody. She was standing on the sidewalk, staring into space.

"What are you doing?" Eddie snapped. "You're supposed to be with us."

Melody didn't answer. Howie tapped her on the shoulder. "Don't you want to get a milk shake?" he asked.

Melody still didn't answer. She stared across the street like she didn't hear her friends. Liza snapped her fingers in front of Melody's face. Melody didn't even blink.

"I don't like this," Liza whined. "She's scaring me."

Howie gulped. "It's like she's in a trance."

"Oh, my gosh," Liza whispered. "What are we going to do?"

2

Patience

"Do something!" Liza told Howie. After all, Howie wanted to be a doctor when he grew up so Liza figured he should know how to wake up someone from a trance.

"I'm trying," Howie said and poked Melody on the shoulder again.

"If she gets stuck like this we can use her as a coatrack," Eddie suggested. "Or we could stick a broom in her hand, wrap a scarf around her neck, and call her a snowman."

"I'll wrap something around your neck," Liza said, "but it will be my hands instead of a scarf! This is nothing to joke about."

Liza grabbed Melody's arms and shook her. Melody jiggled back and forth so hard her black pigtails slapped Liza on the nose. But Melody stood still, staring across the street as if her friends weren't even there.

"What are we going to do?" Liza cried. "Melody has turned into a zombie."

"Wait," Eddie said. "I have an idea." Eddie dug inside his backpack. He pulled out a crumpled math paper, two tennis balls, a huge roll of silver tape, and a long green feather. He threw the paper, tape, and balls to the ground. Then he held up the feather and grinned. "Watch the professional tickler at work," he said.

Liza and Howie stood back as Eddie took the green feather and rubbed it under Melody's chin. Melody smiled, then she giggled. Finally, Melody laughed so hard tears ran down her face.

"Stop," Melody begged as she gasped for breath.

Liza hugged Melody. "We were worried about you," she said. "We thought you turned into a zombie."

"Thank goodness Eddie's tickling scheme worked," Howie said. "What was wrong with you?"

Melody looked at her friends. "I couldn't stop breathing in that wonderful smell."

"All that deep breathing must have gone to your head," Eddie said, "and turned your brains into pumpkin pie."

"That's it!" Melody screamed. "That smell is pumpkin pie and it's coming from over there." Melody pointed to a small store across the street.

Liza read the sign painted on the door: BONSAI BAKERY.

"That wasn't there yesterday," Howie said. "I wonder who owns it."

"Whoever it is," Melody said, taking a deep breath, "they sure know how to make pumpkin pies."

"How do you know?" Eddie said. "You haven't even seen a pumpkin pie."

"You're right," Melody said, looking both ways and hurrying across the street, "but I'm about to eat a whole one right now!"

Liza, Howie, and Eddie followed her. They stopped as soon as they got inside the shop. Bonsai Bakery was deathly still.

"Maybe no one's home," Liza whispered.

"Don't be silly," Melody said. "If nobody was here, the door would be locked."

The four friends looked around the small store. The display case was totally empty, but the walls were filled with beautiful paintings of mountains and dragons. Japanese writing decorated several of them. Tiny trees with crooked branches lined the front windows.

"I know what these are," Liza said. "They're called bonsai trees."

"Those are too small to be trees," Eddie said.

"They're very special trees," she said. "Some people consider them to be works

of art, and it takes great patience to grow trees like that."

"Patience is one thing I don't have," Melody said. "I want a piece of pumpkin pie, and I want it right now!"

"Thanksgiving is just two days away," Liza said. "You can eat all the pumpkin pie you want then."

"I can't wait that long," Melody said.

"Well, it looks like you're going to have to wait," Howie told her, "because the baker is missing."

"Not for long," Melody said. Before her friends could stop her, Melody slid behind the counter and headed for the curtain to the back room.

"You shouldn't be back there," Liza warned. "You could get in trouble."

Melody didn't listen. She marched toward the curtain and pushed it aside. What she saw made her freeze like a Popsicle.

3

Family Secret

"Shhh," Melody warned as her friends crept up behind her and peered over her shoulder. "Don't let him hear us."

"Who is that?" Howie asked. "And what is he doing?

A man with black hair, dressed in loose black pants and a matching shirt, was moving so slowly it looked as if he were swimming in pudding.

"I know what he's doing," Eddie whispered. "He's practicing martial arts moves."

"I thought karate was faster than that," Liza said.

"He's not doing karate," Eddie said.

"How do you know?" Melody asked.

"It looks more like ninjutsu," Eddie explained. "Ancient Japanese warriors

13

practiced ninjutsu. It means 'stealth' and takes great control and patience."

Howie, Liza, and Melody stared at Eddie like he'd just spoken in Japanese. "How do you know all that?" Liza asked.

Eddie shrugged his shoulders. "I know lots of stuff," he bragged. "I've checked out the martial arts books six times from the library."

"I've never seen anyone move like that before," Howie said, staring at the man making slow chopping motions in the air.

"It looks like he's been practicing more than slow-motion moves," Melody said and licked her lips as she stared at the rows and rows of freshly baked pumpkin pies lining the walls of the back room.

Just then, the baker slowly took a step and turned in their direction.

"Ooops," Eddie said and ducked down behind Liza.

Melody cleared her throat. "How do you do?" she said in her most polite

14

voice. "I hope we didn't startle you. My name is Melody and these are my friends Liza, Howie, and Eddie."

Howie smiled and Liza said hello. Eddie waved from his hiding place behind Liza.

The man in black bowed. Then he stood up straight and smiled. "I admire your ability to walk as silently as the clouds floating high above the mountains."

His voice was soft and slow, and he spoke with a distinct accent. "My name," he said, "is Micky Yo. Welcome to the Bonsai Bakery."

Melody smiled. "We smelled those pumpkin pies halfway across Bailey City," she said. "I have never smelled anything so wonderful."

"Would you like to try a piece?" Mr. Yo asked.

"I thought you'd never ask," Melody said.

Mr. Yo reached for a white jacket hanging on a nearby hook. He carefully slipped it over his black shirt and buttoned it up. Then he placed a tall chef's hat on top of his head.

"Now he looks just like a baker is supposed to look," Liza whispered.

"But that's not a normal baker's knife," Howie said.

Liza looked at Mr. Yo and gasped. The new baker was getting ready to slice one of his pies, but instead of a knife he held a long, curved saber high above his head. "Hi-yah!" Mr. Yo yelled. Then he swung the saber down toward the pie. He moved so fast the saber was a blur, but when he was finished the pie was cut into eight perfect slices.

"Wow," Liza said. "You're pretty good with that thing."

Mr. Yo bowed and handed her a slice of pie. Then he gave the other three friends each a piece.

"Mmmm," Liza said as she took a bite. "This is even better than it smells."

Melody nodded. "I've never tasted anything so wonderful. Is that the recipe?" Melody took a step toward a yellowed piece of paper on the counter. But before she reached it, Mr. Yo's saber arched through the air and pinned the recipe to the wooden counter.

"This recipe," Mr. Yo said in a very serious voice, "is a family secret from my home in the rugged mountains of Japan. And I will do anything," he warned, "to protect it!"

4

Ninja

"Hee-hah!" Eddie yelled as they walked down Forest Lane. He jumped up in the air and did a karate chop and kick. "Did you see that Micky Yo? He is so cool. I wonder if I could get a saber like that for Christmas."

Liza sighed. "I don't think sharp weapons are good toys — especially for you," she said.

"Let's just enjoy Thanksgiving first," Melody suggested. "Christmas is still a long way away."

Howie nodded. "I know I'll enjoy Thanksgiving if I get to eat pie like that. I'm going to ask my mom to buy five of them. They were delicious."

"I'm not waiting for my mom to buy one," Melody said. "I'm going to raid my

piggy bank. I love those pies! They taste almost magical."

Eddie stopped beside the street sign and looked at his friends. "I have to tell you something about Micky Yo," Eddie whispered.

"What?" Liza asked.

Eddie looked around and waited for a man walking down the street to pass before speaking. "Those pies probably are magical," Eddie said. "After all, they were made by a ninja."

Melody scratched her head. "What is a ninja?" she asked.

"Ninjas were regular people in Japan," Eddie told his friends. "But they learned to protect themselves. They were so secretive that people started thinking they were magical."

"Maybe they are magical," Melody said softly.

"And," Eddie said, "Micky Yo was dressed exactly like the ninja I saw in the encyclopedia."

"Now I know you're lying," Howie said. "When have you ever looked in an encyclopedia?"

"I'm not lying," Eddie snapped. "My grandmother makes me look at encyclopedias sometimes when I'm in trouble," Eddie explained. "They have some cool stuff in them, even if they are books. I liked the ninja stuff."

Liza put her hands on her hips. "Just because your encyclopedia had a picture of a ninja doesn't mean Mr. Yo is one."

22

"That's right," Howie agreed. "He's just a baker."

"A very good baker," Melody added.

"I think it's a good idea to stay away from this baker," Liza said. "It *was* a little weird how he chopped up that pie. And if he *is* a ninja he could be dangerous."

Howie laughed. "Don't worry. Ninjas are a thing of the past. I'm pretty sure that ninjas don't live in Bailey City, and I'm definitely sure that ninjas don't bake pumpkin pies."

Eddie stamped his foot. "I know a ninja when I see one. Maybe I'll just go back to that bakery tomorrow and find out the truth about Micky Yo."

5

The Letter N

"Here it is," Eddie said the next day after school, pulling a big *N* encyclopedia out of his backpack.

Liza, Howie, and Melody crowded around Eddie. They were on the playground under the oak tree as Eddie turned to the page marked "Ninja." Sure enough, the picture showed a man dressed just like Micky Yo. Eddie smiled. "See, I told you," he said.

"But why would a ninja be in Bailey City?" Liza asked.

"Maybe he came to spy on all the crazy adults we have here," Melody suggested.

"I'm scared," Liza whimpered. "What if Mr. Yo uses his ninja methods to do something bad to Bailey City?"

"Don't worry," Howie said. "There's nothing here that a ninja would want."

"I don't care about ninjas," Melody told her friends. "I just want more of that delicious pumpkin pie."

Liza grabbed Melody's arm. "Don't go back to that bakery," Liza warned. "Something awful might happen."

Eddie laughed. "You read too many scary Halloween books. Maybe if we go back there Micky Yo will teach me some cool ninja moves."

"I'm not going near that bakery," Liza said, folding her arms over her chest.

"Then you'll miss out on a piece of delicious pie," Melody said.

Eddie, Howie, and Melody headed down the street. Liza stood under the oak tree, watching them go. "I hope they'll be all right," she said to herself.

Howie, Melody, and Eddie walked inside the bakery. This time Micky Yo was behind the counter, putting whipped cream on a pie. "Greetings, young ones," Micky Yo said. "Welcome to my bakery."

Melody looked around at the sparkling white walls and shining blue floors. Glass refrigerators held cartons of milk and juices. Everything was very clean, even the shelf holding the bonsai trees. "It is a very nice bakery," Melody said.

Micky Yo wiped his hands on a towel. "This store has brought me much peace and happiness. For me, baking a pie is like creating a sculpture. Every pie is a piece of art."

"They are the best pies I have ever tasted," Howie said. "My mom gave me money to buy three."

Melody put her backpack up on the counter. Her backpack jingled. "I raided my piggy bank," she explained. "I have enough to buy two pies."

Micky Yo smiled and quickly put the pies into boxes for the kids. "It is my pleasure to make pies for customers as polite as you."

"Thank you," Melody said. "It will be my pleasure eating these."

"I liked your pies, too," Eddie said, "but what I really want is for you to teach me something."

"What information do you require?" Micky Yo asked with a smile.

Eddie grinned. "I want to learn some of your ninja moves."

Micky Yo stopped smiling and walked over to the window. He pulled the shades down. When he turned around he looked serious. Dead serious.

6

Close Call

The aroma of pumpkin and cinnamon made Melody's, Eddie's, and Howie's heads dizzy. It felt like their feet were stuck in three feet of cake icing as Micky Yo stepped closer and closer. The kids were frozen to the spot.

Suddenly, the front door to Bonsai Bakery flew open. A chill November wind swept away the sweet smell of Micky Yo's pies as Liza hurried inside.

Micky Yo looked like he was ready to pounce, but Liza spoke before he had a chance. "You have to come with me," she lied to her friends. "I heard your mothers calling for you."

Melody, Howie, and Eddie grabbed their pies and quickly dodged Micky Yo

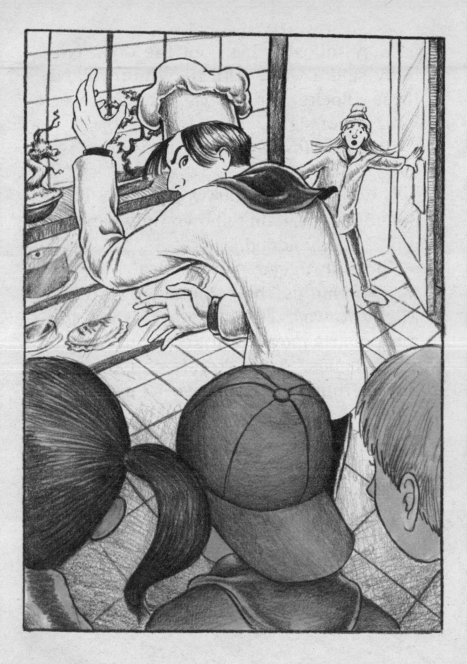

as they followed Liza out the door. No-body said a word until they had walked three blocks and Bonsai Bakery was long out of sight.

"Whew," Howie said. "That was a close call."

"I don't know what would have hap-pened if Liza hadn't shown up when she did," Melody added.

Eddie shrugged. "I'm mad at Liza for interrupting us," he complained. "I think Micky Yo was getting ready to show me martial arts moves that I could use on all my enemies." Eddie karate-chopped the air in front of Liza's nose to prove his point.

Howie nodded. "Sure he was," he said. "Moves like tossing you over his head and clear across the bakery."

"Micky Yo wouldn't do anything like that," Eddie argued. "Even if he is a ninja, we have nothing to worry about."

"Yes we do," Liza interrupted. "I think I found out why a ninja would come to

Bailey City, and if I'm right, we all need to worry."

"What are you talking about?" Melody said.

"I'll show you," Liza said as she pulled her friends down the sidewalk toward the Bailey City library. Six gargoyles glared down at the kids from the roof as Liza led her friends up the steps to the front door. "There it is," she said. "Proof that Mr. Yo is a ninja." Melody, Howie, and Eddie looked where Liza pointed. A piece of paper taped to the door flapped in the breeze. Eddie stepped closer and snatched it down. Then he held it so his friends could see.

"This is about the Shelley Museum," he said. "It has nothing to do with the new baker in town."

"You're wrong," Liza said. "Look closer."

Howie grabbed the flyer from Eddie. "There's an art exhibit at the museum," Howie said.

"Exactly," Liza said. "Now you're getting it."

"The only thing I'm getting is mad, mad, MAD," Eddie told her. "You're not making any sense!"

Liza took the paper from Howie and pointed to the small print at the bottom of the page. "It says the exhibit is of rare Japanese art, some of which is priceless," she explained to her friends. "I think Micky Yo is here to steal that art."

"I wonder if that art is as rare as the brains in your head?" Eddie mumbled.

"Why would a pumpkin pie wizard want to steal Japanese art?" Melody asked.

Liza shook her head. "I don't know, but it's up to us to stop him!"

7

The Shelley Museum

Eddie and Melody bumped heads as Eddie's grandmother drove over the bridge leading to the Shelley Museum of Art and Science. Melody rubbed her forehead. "Your head is even harder than I thought," she complained.

"Don't blame me," Eddie said. "It's all Liza's fault that we're even here."

Liza, Melody, Howie, and Eddie sat in the back of the van. They spoke in whispers so Eddie's grandmother wouldn't hear.

"Visiting the museum won't hurt you," Liza said.

"You're wrong," Eddie snapped. "It's already given me a headache, and we haven't even gotten there yet."

"Liza's right," Melody said. "We've

never seen art like this before. It may be interesting."

"I have better things to do than to stare at a bunch of drawings hanging in a stuffy museum," Eddie told her.

"Art is much more than drawing," Howie told Eddie. "Paintings and sculptures — even tools — are all art forms."

Liza nodded. "You don't have to go to a museum to find art, either. It's in the gargoyles on top of the library; it's in the gardens at the park. Art is everywhere."

"And it tells a story," Melody added. "You just have to figure it out."

"I've figured out one thing already," Eddie said. "All my friends are as nutty as peanut butter cookies."

"Mmmm," Liza said. "A cookie sounds good."

"I'd pass up an entire tray of cookies for just one of Mr. Yo's pies," Melody said. "He was right when he said his pies were like art."

Liza gulped. "Mr. Yo's bakery definitely

has art," she reminded them all. "He has paintings on the walls, and the windows are lined with bonsai trees. If we don't do something fast, he'll have all the art from Bailey City, too."

"I hope you're wrong," Howie said, "because a city without art would be very boring."

The van stirred up a cloud of dust as Eddie's grandmother turned down the dirt road leading to the museum. When the van stopped, they all climbed out. Leaves from nearby giant oak trees blew across the brown grass and clung to the cuffs of their jeans and got tangled in their shoestrings. The kids stood, staring up at the Shelley Museum as Eddie's grandmother walked toward the front door.

The old building sat on top of a hill. A broken shutter slapped against the peeling paint of the woodwork. Dark winter clouds hung low in the sky.

Liza shivered and Howie pulled his

jacket tight. "It hasn't changed a bit," he said with a shaky voice.

This wasn't the first time they had been to the museum. They all remembered the field trip they took with their third-grade class. That's when they met Dr. Victor, the museum director, and his assistant, Frank. The kids were sure Dr. Victor was a mad scientist and that Frank was really the Frankenstein monster.

"Maybe Eddie was right," Melody said. "This isn't a good idea."

"Are you coming?" Eddie's grandmother yelled cheerfully from the museum's door. "Time's a-wasting!"

Liza took a deep breath. "We'll be safe," she told her friends. "After all, Eddie's grandmother won't let anything bad happen to us."

"It's too late for me," Eddie said with a sigh. "I'm already doomed. Grandma was so excited when I asked her to bring us to the museum, I bet she's already planning to take me to every museum within a hundred miles."

"It could be worse," Liza said. "You'll have to go even farther if evil ninjas take all the art in Bailey City."

Then Liza led her friends up the crumbling steps leading to the heavy wooden door of the museum. The door creaked open and Eddie's grandmother waited until they were all inside before letting the door close with a definite thud.

8

Samurai

The museum was silent as they followed the signs for the art exhibit. They passed one room lined with mummies, another room that looked like the inside of a cave, and a third room filled with dinosaur bones.

"I'm glad your grandmother knows her way around," Melody said. "It'd be very easy to get lost in this maze of hallways."

Liza nodded, remembering when she and Melody took a wrong turn during their last visit and ended up in Dr. Victor's secret laboratory.

"Here we are," Eddie's grandmother said as she led them into a large room.

One side of the room was filled with beautiful paintings of mountains, waterfalls, and forests. Down the center of the room stood silk screens filled with scenes of flowers and birds. Porcelain vases and bowls lined shelves on the far side of the exhibit. Silk kimonos dangled from the ceiling. Signs explaining the art hung by each piece.

"These are wonderful," Melody said.

"They show the beauty of the land," Howie added.

"That's not all they show," Liza said as she led her friends to a corner exhibit where the watercolor paintings were filled with scowling warriors swinging swords.

"That's just like the sword Micky Yo used to slice his pumpkin pies," Melody reminded them.

A glass case next to the paintings held silver stars with deadly jagged edges. A coiled rope with hooks hung below the stars.

Liza nodded. "This sign says the pieces in this part of the exhibit came from a period of time when the samurai controlled the largest island of Japan, called Honshu. Everyone had to do what the samurai told them to do."

"That sounds like the teachers at Bailey School," Eddie said with a nod.

"Except the samurai were skilled warriors," Liza pointed out.

"Sometimes I think teachers are worse than sword-swinging warriors," Eddie grumbled.

Howie pointed to a small paragraph printed at the bottom of the sign. "Ac-

NETSUKE

cording to this, not everybody followed the samurai," he read to his friends. "A group of people fled from the samurai and their unfair rulers. This exhibit includes priceless art left behind when they fled to the mountains. This rebel group of people learned to use the power of the mountains, trees, water, and even fire. They would not hesitate to use their new skills of warfare and spying to protect themselves and their families. They even trained special warriors called

genin. These people became known as the ninja and the secret ways they used to increase their personal power were called *Mikkyo*."

"Oh, no!" Liza squealed so loudly a group of people turned to stare at the kids.

"Shhh," Melody warned. "You'll get us thrown out of the museum."

"LA! LA! LA!" Eddie sang at the top of his lungs.

Howie clamped his hand over Eddie's mouth. "What are you doing?" Howie asked. He moved his hand just a little so Eddie could answer.

"I'm trying to get us thrown out of the museum," he told Howie.

"We can't get thrown out," Liza warned. "Because this is much worse than I thought."

"You're absolutely right," Eddie said. "Standing in a museum looking at pictures of birds and trees is definitely worse than my scariest nightmare."

"That's not what I'm talking about," Liza said. "Don't you know what all this means? Samurai stole the ancient art in this exhibit, and now the ninjas have sent their most powerful *genin* warrior to get it back. And his name is *Micky Yo!*"

"So what?" Eddie said. "According to this, the art belonged to the ninjas in the first place."

"The problem," Liza said seriously, "is that the samurai aren't going to be willing to give it up."

"What are you getting at?" Melody asked like she didn't really want to know.

Liza looked around to make sure no one was listening before answering. "If I'm right, then Bailey City might be caught right in the middle of a war between a samurai warrior and a ninja *genin!*"

9

Secret Weapon

"What samurai?" Eddie asked. "I haven't seen anybody wearing crazy hats like those dudes in the pictures."

Liza wouldn't back down. "If a ninja is stealing art, I'm sure there's a samurai not far behind."

Melody patted Liza on the arm. "Why don't we just relax and look at the stuff in the museum? It looks interesting."

Liza sighed but followed her friends as they looked around. Eddie's grandmother was already at the far end of the big room looking at paintings when Liza pointed to a piece of wood carved into hundreds of tiny people. "Oh, my gosh," Liza exclaimed. "How could anyone ever do anything like that?"

The kids stared at the wood in amazement. "I bet I could carve something like that," Eddie bragged, "if my grandmother would just buy me a pocketknife."

Melody rolled her eyes. "Your grandmother would have to be insane to buy you a sharp knife."

Liza nodded. "You might poke your eye out."

"I would not," Eddie snapped, his face turning as red as his hair. Eddie was so mad, he didn't even notice the dark figure sliding up behind him. Liza, Howie, and Melody noticed, though. They stared and pointed behind Eddie, but none of them could speak.

Finally, Howie managed to squeak, "Mi-mi."

"What's wrong?" Eddie asked. "Samurai got your tongue?"

Howie shook his head and stammered, "B-behind you."

Eddie turned around and poked his nose right into a black shirt. Eddie gulped and looked up into the grinning

face of Micky Yo. "I see you are enjoying the exhibit," Micky Yo said.

The kids nodded and Micky Yo moved on to look at the samurai swords. Liza pulled her friends to the end of the room and whispered, "I bet he's here to steal some of the art."

Howie nodded. "He does seem fascinated by the swords."

"Maybe we should warn someone he's here," Melody suggested, "just in case."

"How about if I try some of my karate moves on him?" Eddie asked, chopping the air. "After all, I did take karate classes for a while."

Liza shook her head and frowned. "No, if Mickey Yo is a real ninja, he knows more moves than all of us put together."

"When I bumped into him, he did have muscles of steel," Eddie admitted.

Liza twisted her hands in front of her. "What should we do?" she worried.

Eddie grinned. "Don't worry," he said, "I never come unprepared."

"What are you talking about?" Howie asked. "You sound like a Boy Scout."

Eddie patted his backpack and said, "I have a secret weapon in here that will take care of any ninja within a hundred miles."

10

Catching a Ninja

"What's the secret weapon?" Melody asked softly, after checking to make sure Mickey Yo wasn't looking.

Eddie reached into his backpack and pulled out a huge roll of silver tape. "What good will tape do?" Liza asked. "We don't need to wrap any presents."

"That tape isn't for wrapping presents," Howie said. "That's duct tape. It's the strongest tape around. My dad even used it one time to stop a leaky pipe."

"But we don't have any leaky pipes around here," Melody said. "Can't we just stop all this craziness and look at the rest of the paintings with your grandmother?"

Eddie shook his head. "Paintings are boring, but catching a ninja is cool."

Liza put her hand on her forehead. "Oh, no," she moaned. "What have I done?"

Eddie ignored Liza and went on to explain his plan. "Here's what we'll do," he said. "Liza will talk to Micky Yo while we sneak up behind him and wrap tape around him."

"Why me?" Liza said with a gulp. "Why do I have to talk to him?"

"Because you're the nicest one," Eddie said matter-of-factly.

"It'll never work," Melody said. "Micky Yo will break the tape before we even get his arms pinned down."

"I don't know," Howie said. "That tape is pretty strong. I think it would even hold a five-ton elephant."

"How do you know?" Eddie asked. "Did you ever have a five-ton elephant stand on that tape?"

Liza giggled as she pictured a huge elephant in a tutu standing on a strip of tape.

Howie shrugged. "Of course not, but I heard it somewhere."

"Elephants don't matter," Melody said. "Ninjas are what we have to think about now."

"Melody's right," Eddie agreed.

"What I want to know," Melody said, "is what happens if your little tape trick doesn't work?"

Eddie looked at Micky Yo and then looked at the duct tape. "Then we're nothing but Thanksgiving turkeys," Eddie said.

11

Fast Action

"Okay," Eddie said, pulling a strip of tape loose. "The first thing we do is tape his mouth shut so he can't yell for help."

"Why would a burglar call for help?" Howie asked.

Melody nodded. "Howie has a point."

Liza crossed her arms over her chest. "We can't do it," she said.

Eddie waved a piece of tape at Liza. "Why can't we?" he asked.

"It's too dangerous," she said. "If we put that tape over Mickey Yo's mouth he might choke."

Eddie rolled his eyes. "There's no way that would happen."

"Liza's right," Howie said. "We have to think of something else."

"And fast," Melody said, pointing

toward Micky Yo. He had a small vase in his hands. He rubbed it with his black shirtsleeve and examined it closely. Then he glanced around the room. When it looked like no one was looking, Micky Yo stuck the tiny vase into his pants pocket.

"Oh, my gosh," Liza squealed. "He really is stealing!"

"Time to go to plan B," Eddie said, running to the exit door. He quickly pulled the tape back and forth over the door, blocking the main exit.

"What are you doing?" Howie asked.

"I'm blocking his escape route while you go for help," Eddie explained as he strapped tape across the doorway.

"We're going to need help," Melody said, "because here comes Micky Yo and he doesn't look happy."

Liza put her hand to her forehead. "I think I'm going to faint."

"Don't worry. I'll save the day," Eddie said. He stood in front of the door and

spread out his arms. "H
the Human Shield!"
Micky Yo headed
direction while
came from a
them were
budge. Ed
quickly
"W
wa

e'll never get past

d for the kids from one
Eddie's grandmother
nother direction. Both of
frowning. But Eddie didn't
die's grandmother moved very
and reached them first.

hat in the world are you doing, Ed-
rd?" his grandmother asked.

Eddie's face turned red at the mention
of his full name. "I — I," Eddie stammered.

"We're catching a thief," Liza said
firmly as she stepped beside Eddie.

Melody and Howie joined their
friends. "We won't let him steal this
priceless art," Melody added.

Micky Yo gasped and turned in a circle.
"Where's a thief?" Micky Yo asked, looking all around.

"You're the thief," Howie said.

Micky Yo frowned at the kids. Then he
stepped closer and closer.

12

Sticky Situation

"You'll never get away with it," Eddie said bravely as Micky Yo came at the four kids.

"A ninja's skill is no match for the Bailey School kids," Melody added. But her voice shook when she said it.

"What on earth are you talking about?" Eddie's grandmother interrupted.

But they didn't have a chance to answer because just then Dr. Victor and his giant assistant, Frank, thundered down the hall and headed straight through the door to the exhibit.

Well, at least they tried to, but they were stopped by Eddie's duct tape like two huge flies in a sticky spiderweb. The more they tried to get free, the more tangled they became.

"Hhhrrrrm!" Frank roared as he struggled against the tape. He swung his huge arms and kicked at the silver web. When he did, a piece of tape pulled loose from the wall, taking a huge chunk of paint with it. The more Frank tore at the tape, the more he ripped paint free from the museum's wall.

"Gadzooks!" Dr. Victor yelled as he tried to pull tape from his beard. "Who is responsible for a monster trap such as this?"

"You can thank us!" Eddie told him proudly. "We just stopped Micky Yo from stealing from your museum!"

Dr. Victor stopped plucking at the tape and glared at Micky Yo. "What's the meaning of this sticky situation?" he asked.

Everybody looked at Mickey Yo as he shrugged and took the vase from his pocket. "This vase has a smudge on it," he told them. "I was going to polish it and bring it back."

"Surely you don't expect us to believe that old story!" Eddie said with a laugh.

"Why shouldn't we believe him?" Dr. Victor asked. "After all, this exhibit belongs to him."

"W-w-what?" Liza gasped.

"That's right," Micky Yo said. "I brought these pieces from my home. They have been in my family for generations."

"Oh my," Eddie's grandmother said. "I believe these children owe you an apology."

"It's too late for apologies," Mickey Yo said seriously. He put the vase down on a nearby table and reached over to snatch a sword from the wall. Then Micky Yo faced the kids.

"Apologies will not repair this damage," he told the kids. "But I know what will."

Liza gulped and hid behind Melody. "I think Eddie's about to see those ninja

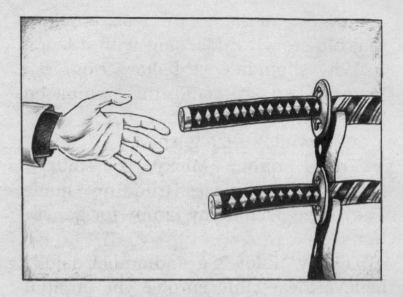

moves he was talking about," Liza whimpered.

Melody nodded. "Like tossing kids across rooms and through windows."

Howie backed up and Melody got ready to duck. But Eddie put his hands in the air, ready to karate chop his way through the duct tape and out the front door of the museum. He never got the chance.

13

Painting at the Museum

Eddie dipped his paintbrush in the bucket. Even though he was trying to be careful he already had three splotches of paint in his hair and a big paint blob on his nose. "I didn't think this was the kind of painting we'd be seeing when you said we were coming to an art exhibit at the museum," Eddie griped.

The museum had closed for the evening and Melody, Liza, Howie, and Eddie were busy painting over the spots torn loose from Eddie's duct tape.

"You have no one to blame but yourself," Melody told him as she painted over another spot.

"Melody's right," Howie said, being careful not to drip any paint on the floor. "If it wasn't for that super-duper tape

67

scheme of yours, we'd be home watching football right now."

"I thought Micky Yo was going to carve us up like a Thanksgiving turkey with that ancient ninja sword," Melody added.

Howie carefully brushed paint over another spot on the wall. "Lucky for us he just used his sword to cut Frank and Dr. Victor free from all of Eddie's tape."

"It's not all my fault," Eddie argued. "Liza's the one who said Micky Yo was a rebel ninja who wanted to steal back his family's missing art."

"That's true," Melody said with a laugh. "I guess we were all pretty silly for thinking Micky Yo was about to battle a samurai warrior right here in Bailey City."

"Especially since there wasn't a samurai warrior around for Micky Yo to fight," Eddie pointed out.

"Unless," Liza said slowly, "the samurai warrior hasn't found Micky Yo hiding out in Bailey City yet."

"But that would mean our ninja troubles aren't over," Melody said. "They're just starting!"

Melody, Howie, and Eddie froze, their paintbrushes in midair.

"Don't be ridiculous," Howie finally said with a nervous laugh.

"After all," Melody said with a gulp, "ninjas don't bake pumpkin pies. Do they?"

Debbie Dadey and Marcia Thornton Jones have fun writing stories together. When they both worked at an elementary school in Lexington, Kentucky, Debbie was the school librarian and Marcia was a teacher. During their lunch break in the school cafeteria, they came up with the idea of the Bailey School kids.

Recently Debbie and her family moved to Aurora, Illinois. Marcia and her husband still live in Kentucky where she continues to teach. How do these authors still write together? They talk on the phone and use computers and fax machines!

Creepy, weird, wacky, and funny things happen to the Bailey School Kids!™ Collect and read them all!

The Adventures of
THE BAILEY SCHOOL KIDS®